ROMANCE & LOVE

PART 2

ECHOES OF ROMANCE, A TREASURE TROVE OF TIMELESS FICTIONAL SHORT STORIES

SOPHIA ISABELLA

ACKNOWLEDGEMENTS

I wish to express my sincere and heartfelt gratitude to all the readers who have embraced this book series of love stories with open hearts and minds. Your support and encouragement have been the driving force behind my writing. I would also like to thank my family and friends for their unwavering support and belief in my abilities. Your love, patience, and understanding have been invaluable in helping us bring these stories to life. Finally, I would like to acknowledge the inspiration that I have drawn from the world of love and relationships. The beauty, complexity, and power of love have been our constant muse, and I am grateful for the opportunity to share my vision of love with you.

©2024 Sophia Isabella. All rights reserved.

INTRODUCTION

Welcome to the book series of short love stories, where every page is filled with the magic and wonder of love in its many forms. Each book in this series contains 20 heartwarming and enchanting tales that explore the diverse and intricate tapestry of human relationships.

From the fiery passion of new love to the enduring commitment of long-term partnerships, from the heartache of lost love to the joy of rediscovered affection, our stories cover a wide range of themes and emotions. We have crafted these tales with the hope of touching your heart and inspiring your soul, offering a glimpse into the beauty and complexity of love in all its forms. Further, from the thrilling excitement of first encounters to the quiet comfort of long-term partnerships, the stories delve into the emotions and experiences that make love such a powerful and transformative force. With themes ranging from heartache and loss to joy and redemption, we have crafted these tales to resonate with readers on a deep and personal level.

Whether you are seeking a romantic escape, a heartfelt connection, or simply a good story to curl up with, we invite you to dive into the world of our short love stories and let the magic of love take you on an unforgettable journey.

CONTENTS

ACKNOWLEDGEMENTS 2
INTRODUCTION 3
CONTENTS 4

- Story 1: A Love That Never Dies 5
- Story 2: The Sweetness of Your Touch 7
- Story 3: The Unspoken Love 9
- Story 4: Whispering Hearts 11
- Story 5: Echoes of Love 13
- Story 6: The Timeless Bond 15
- Story 7: A Love That Conquers All 17
- Story 8: A Love That Sparkles 19
- Story 9: A Love That Takes Flight 21
- Story 10: A Love Beyond Time 23
- Story 11: Moonlit Promises 25
- Story 12: The Pureness of Love 27
- Story 13: The Timeless Passion 29
- Story 14: Love at First Sight 31
- Story 15: The Perfect Match 34
- Story 16: A Boundless Love 37
- Story 17: The Sweetness of Your Kiss 39
- Story 18: A Love That Heals 41
- Story 19: The Serene Bliss of Love 43
- Story 20: The Heart's Secret 45

Story 1: A Love That Never Dies

In the picturesque town of Savannah, Georgia, lived a young woman named Clara Williams. Clara was known for her compassionate nature and her infectious laughter, which could brighten even the darkest days. She worked as a nurse at the local hospital, dedicating her life to helping others.

One sunny afternoon, Clara was taking a break in the hospital's garden, enjoying the warmth of the sun on her face. She heard footsteps approaching and turned to see a tall, ruggedly handsome man with kind eyes and a charming smile. His name was Ethan Miller, a war veteran who had recently been admitted to the hospital for treatment of a severe injury he received during his service.

Ethan had been through a lot, both physically and emotionally, but Clara's warmth and kindness touched his heart in a way he hadn't experienced in a long time. They began to talk, sharing stories of their pasts and dreams for the future. Clara was captivated by Ethan's strength and resilience, while Ethan was drawn to her compassion and sense of humor.

As time went on, Clara and Ethan's friendship blossomed into something deeper. They spent every moment they could together, whether it was walking through the garden, watching movies, or simply sitting and talking. Clara's laughter became the soundtrack of Ethan's recovery, and he found himself falling in love with her in a way he never thought possible.

But life had a way of throwing curveballs, and Ethan's injury was more severe than initially thought. Despite Clara's tireless efforts to help him, his condition worsened, and the doctors had to inform him that his chances of survival were slim.

Ethan was devastated, but he didn't want to face his final days without Clara. He asked her to marry him, wanting to spend eternity with her in every way possible. Clara, tears streaming down her face, said yes without hesitation. They were married in a small, intimate ceremony in the hospital garden, surrounded by their closest friends and family.

Ethan's condition continued to decline, and it wasn't long before he was bedridden, unable to move or speak. Clara never left his side, holding his hand, whispering words of love and encouragement, and playing their favorite songs to bring him comfort.

One quiet evening, as the sun dipped below the horizon, Ethan's breathing became labored. Clara knew that his time was near, and she held him tighter, her tears mingling with his. As he took his last breath, Clara whispered, "I love you, Ethan. Until we meet again."

Months passed, and Clara struggled to find peace in the wake of her loss. She threw herself into her work, but nothing could fill the void left by Ethan's absence. She often found herself wandering through the garden, remembering their happy moments and feeling his presence in the breeze.

One day, as Clara was walking through the garden, she saw a butterfly fluttering above the flowers. It was a monarch butterfly, Ethan's favorite. She watched it for a moment, feeling a sense of calm wash over her.

From that day on, Clara began to see monarch butterflies everywhere she went. They seemed to follow her, as if guiding her through the grieving process. She found comfort in their presence, feeling like Ethan was still with her, watching over her, and loving her from beyond.

Years went by, and Clara's heart began to heal. She never forgot Ethan, and she knew that their love would never die. She continued to work as a nurse, spreading her compassion and kindness to everyone she met, just as Ethan had done in his own way.

One day, as Clara was taking a walk through the garden, she saw a young couple sitting on a bench, holding hands and smiling. The man had a kind smile and eyes that sparkled with joy, just like Ethan's. Clara felt a sense of peace wash over her, knowing that love, like the monarch butterflies, transcends time and space.

And so, Clara lived her life with a heart full of love, knowing that Ethan was always with her, guiding her, and loving her, just as he had promised. Their love was eternal, a testament to the power of true love that never dies.

Story 2: The Sweetness of Your Touch

In the small town of Rosewood, California, lived a young woman named Emily Johnson. Emily was a talented baker, known for her delicious pastries and treats that could bring a smile to anyone's face. She worked at a quaint bakery called "Sugar & Spice," where she created magical confections that people came from all over to taste.

One sunny morning, as Emily was setting up for the day, she noticed a tall, charming man standing at the counter, admiring her creations. His name was Jack Thompson, a new resident of Rosewood who had recently moved to the area to start a fresh chapter in his life.

Jack was immediately drawn to Emily's warm smile and the sweet aroma of her baked goods. He ordered a slice of her famous apple pie and found himself captivated by its delicious flavor and the way it made him feel. He decided to come back to Sugar & Spice every day, hoping to catch a glimpse of Emily and taste her incredible pastries.

Emily, too, found herself drawn to Jack. His kind eyes and charming demeanor made her feel at ease, and she enjoyed their conversations about life, dreams, and of course, baked goods. As time went on, their friendship blossomed into something deeper, and they soon found themselves falling in love.

Jack was a talented artist, and he began to paint pictures of Emily and her bakery, capturing the essence of her joy and creativity. Emily, in turn, began to bake treats inspired by Jack's paintings, creating delicious works of art that they could share and enjoy together.

One special day, Jack surprised Emily with a painting of her, holding a tray of her famous pastries, with the bakery's name "Sugar & Spice" written in elegant script above her head. Emily was touched by the gesture, and she knew that Jack was the one for her.

As their love grew, they found themselves creating magical moments together, whether it was baking in the bakery, painting in Jack's studio, or simply sitting on the porch of their cozy home, watching the sunset and enjoying each other's company.

But life had a way of throwing curveballs, and Emily was diagnosed with a rare illness that affected her ability to taste and smell. She was devastated by the news, feeling like she had lost a part of herself that was essential to her baking and her relationship with Jack.

Jack, however, refused to let Emily's illness come between them. He was determined to find a way to bring back the sweetness that had always been a part of their love. He began to research and experiment with different spices and flavors, trying to find a way to create treats that Emily could enjoy despite her condition.

After many trials and errors, Jack finally created a special blend of spices and flavors that he called "The Sweetness of Your Touch." The blend was inspired by Emily's warmth, kindness, and creativity, and it had a unique, unforgettable flavor that brought joy to anyone who tasted it.

Emily was touched by Jack's efforts, and she found herself falling in love with him all over again. She couldn't taste the treats the way she once did, but she could feel the love and care that went into each one, and that was enough for her.

Years went by, and Emily and Jack continued to create magical moments together, sharing their love and passion for baking and art. They opened a new bakery together, called "The Sweetness of Your Touch," where they shared their delicious treats and the story of their love with everyone who came through their doors.

Emily and Jack's love was a testament to the power of true love and the sweetness that comes from being with someone who truly cares. They knew that no matter what life threw at them, they would always have each other, and that was enough to make their hearts feel full and happy.

Story 3: The Unspoken Love

In the bustling city of New York, lived a young woman named Clara Williams. Clara was a talented photographer, known for her ability to capture the beauty and essence of life in her photographs. She worked as a freelance photographer, taking on various projects and assignments that allowed her to travel and explore the world.

One day, Clara was assigned to photograph a charity event in Brooklyn, where she met a charming and kind-hearted man named David Lee. David was a volunteer at the event, helping to organize and coordinate the various activities. He was immediately drawn to Clara's passion for photography and her ability to capture the true essence of the people and moments she photographed.

Clara, too, found herself drawn to David. His kindness, generosity, and passion for helping others made him stand out in the crowd. They struck up a conversation, and Clara found herself sharing her love for photography and her dreams of traveling the world to capture its beauty. David, in turn, shared his own dreams and aspirations, and they soon found themselves forming a deep and meaningful connection.

As time went on, Clara and David continued to see each other, meeting up for coffee, going on walks in the park, and sharing their thoughts and feelings with one another. They never spoke of their feelings for each other, but their actions and the way they treated each other spoke volumes.

Clara would often take David's picture, capturing the warmth and kindness in his eyes, while David would always make sure to bring Clara's favorite coffee and pastries when they met up. They would sit and talk for hours, sharing their dreams, fears, and hopes for the future, and finding comfort and solace in each other's presence.

One day, Clara was assigned to photograph a remote village in the mountains of Peru. She was excited for the opportunity to travel and capture the beauty of a new place, but she was also sad to be leaving David behind. They promised to stay in touch and share their experiences with each other, but Clara knew that being apart would be difficult.

While in Peru, Clara found herself missing David more than she had ever thought possible. She took pictures of the stunning landscape and the people she met, but she couldn't shake the feeling that she was missing something important. She realized that what she was missing was David, and the unspoken love that had grown between them.

When Clara returned to New York, she was eager to see David and tell him how much he meant to her. She found him waiting for her at the airport, holding a bouquet of her favorite flowers and a warm smile. They embraced, and Clara knew that she had never been happier.

From that moment on, Clara and David's love grew stronger and deeper, and they knew that they had found something special in each other. They continued to share their lives and dreams, traveling the world together and capturing its beauty through Clara's lens.

Their love was unspoken, but it was powerful and real. They knew that they had found something truly special in each other, and they cherished every moment they spent together. Clara and David's love was a testament to the beauty of unspoken feelings and the power of a deep and meaningful connection.

Story 4: Whispering Hearts

In the quaint town of Maplewood, nestled in the heart of Vermont, love bloomed in the most unexpected ways. It was here that Emily Parker and Liam O'Connor's paths were destined to intertwine, their hearts whispering secrets to one another before they ever met.

Emily, with her cascading auburn hair and eyes that sparkled like the morning dew, worked at the local bookstore, "Literature Lane." She had a passion for reading and a knack for recommending the perfect book to anyone who crossed her path. Her days were filled with the aroma of freshly printed pages and the soothing sound of turning pages.

Liam, on the other hand, was a talented musician with a heart full of melodies and a soul that yearned for expression. He played the guitar at "The Rustic Roost," a cozy café that doubled as a live music venue every Friday night. His songs, filled with raw emotion and a hint of blues, resonated deeply with the townsfolk.

Their worlds collided on a crisp autumn evening. Emily had just closed up shop at Literature Lane and decided to treat herself to a warm cup of chamomile tea at The Rustic Roost. As she entered, the soft glow of fairy lights and the gentle hum of conversation enveloped her. She spotted an empty table near the window and settled in, savoring the quiet before the evening's entertainment began.

Liam, nervous yet excited, took the stage. He had been composing a new song, inspired by the fleeting moments of connection he had witnessed in Maplewood. As his fingers danced across the guitar strings, the melody flowed like a gentle stream, carrying words that seemed to have been written just for Emily.
"In a town where whispers carry tales,
Of dreams and hearts that dare to sail,
I found a face, a glance so bright,
That lit up my darkest night."

Emily's eyes widened as she recognized the subtle nod to Literature Lane in his lyrics. She felt a connection, a pull, that she couldn't quite explain. By the time Liam finished his set, she was on her feet, applauding with all her heart.

Their first conversation was awkward yet enchanting. Liam approached her table, shyly asking if she enjoyed the song. Emily smiled warmly, her eyes reflecting the admiration she felt for his talent. They spoke of books, music, and the simple joys of living in Maplewood. Before they knew it, the café had emptied, and they were still there, lost in each other's company.

As the weeks passed, their friendship blossomed into something deeper. They took long walks through the colorful autumn leaves, shared cups of coffee at dawn, and spent countless hours talking about their dreams and fears. Emily found herself looking forward to Liam's sets more than anything, and Liam's music seemed to grow richer, more soulful, with Emily in his life.

One snowy evening, as Maplewood was blanketed in a pristine layer of white, Liam invited Emily to a secret spot he had discovered—a small, frozen pond nestled between two hills. He had brought his guitar and a blanket, planning to share something special with her.

As they sat huddled together, the moonlight casting a silvery glow on the snow, Liam began to play. This time, the song was one he had written specifically for Emily.
"Whispering hearts, in syncopated rhymes,
Two souls, entwined by silent binds,
In this quiet town, where love finds its way,
Together, we'll dance through life's endless play."

Emily's eyes filled with tears as she realized the depth of Liam's feelings. She reached out, her fingers tracing the outline of his hand. "Liam," she whispered, "my heart has been whispering your name since the first night I heard you play."

And there, under the moonlight, surrounded by the whispers of the snow, their hearts finally confessed what their eyes had known all along. They embraced, their love as pure and unspoken as the falling snow, yet as powerful as the melodies Liam played.

From that night on, Emily and Liam became an inseparable part of Maplewood's fabric. Their love story, like the whispering hearts they once were, spread through the town, inspiring others to believe in the magic of unexpected connections. And in the quiet corners of Literature Lane and The Rustic Roost, their story lived on, a testament to the beauty of love that blooms when two souls find each other in the most unassuming of places.

Story 5: Echoes of Love

In the picturesque town of Evergreen, nestled in the rolling hills of North Carolina, love had a way of echoing through the generations. It was here that Sarah Mitchell and Jackson Brown, two souls destined to find each other, discovered that love had a language all its own—one that transcended time and space.

Sarah, with her cascading chestnut hair and eyes that sparkled like the morning dew, was a historical preservationist with a passion for Evergreen's rich past. She spent her days restoring old buildings and uncovering forgotten stories, her heart always attuned to the whispers of the past.

Jackson, a tall and rugged man with a heart as vast as the Carolina sky, was a contemporary artist with a penchant for capturing the essence of life in his paintings. His studio, nestled in the heart of Evergreen, was filled with vivid landscapes and portraits that seemed to breathe with the spirit of the town.

Their worlds collided on a crisp autumn day when Sarah approached Jackson to discuss the restoration of an old church that stood at the edge of town. The building, known as St. Cecilia's, was a historical gem, but it had fallen into disrepair over the years. Jackson, intrigued by the challenge, agreed to help, and together they embarked on a journey that would change their lives forever.

As they worked side by side, Sarah and Jackson's bond grew stronger. They spoke of their dreams, fears, and the stories that shaped them. Sarah shared her love for Evergreen's history, while Jackson revealed his fascination with capturing its spirit. They discovered a shared passion for the town and its people, a connection that seemed to resonate with the echoes of love that had once been felt by those who walked its streets.

One evening, as they were wrapping up for the day, Jackson revealed a painting he had been working on—a portrait of Sarah, her eyes filled with the same sparkle as the old photographs he had seen in St. Cecilia's. The painting captured her essence perfectly, her love for Evergreen shining through in every brushstroke.

Sarah was moved beyond words. She had never felt so seen, so understood. She reached out, her fingers tracing the outline of her face in the painting. "Jackson," she whispered, "this... this is me."

Jackson smiled, his eyes reflecting the same depth of feeling. "It's not just you, Sarah. It's all of us. Evergreen, its history, its people... they're all in this painting. And in you."

From that moment on, their relationship deepened. They spent countless hours exploring the town, uncovering its secrets, and creating new memories. They painted murals on the sides of buildings, restored old furniture, and organized community events that brought the town together.

One snowy winter evening, as Evergreen was blanketed in a pristine layer of white, Jackson took Sarah to a secret spot he had discovered—a small, frozen pond nestled between two hills. He had brought his easel and paints, planning to capture the beauty of the moment.

As they stood together, the moonlight casting a silvery glow on the snow, Jackson began to paint. This time, the painting was one he had dreamed of for months—a portrait of Sarah and Evergreen, intertwined in a dance of love and history.

Sarah watched in awe as Jackson's brushstrokes brought the scene to life. She saw herself, her love for the town, and the echoes of love that had once been felt by those who had walked its streets. She saw the future they could build together, a future rooted in the past but reaching toward the infinite possibilities of the present.

When Jackson finally finished, he turned to Sarah, his eyes filled with love and hope. "Sarah," he whispered, "this painting... it's our story. It's the echo of love that has always been here, waiting for us to find it."

Sarah's eyes filled with tears as she realized the truth of his words. She reached out, her hand finding Jackson's, and together they stood, their hearts echoing with the love that had always been there, waiting to be discovered.

From that night on, Sarah and Jackson's love became an enduring part of Evergreen's story. Their bond, like the echoes of love that had once been felt by those who walked its streets, resonated through the generations, inspiring others to believe in the magic of love that transcends time and space.

Story 6: The Timeless Bond

In the charming town of Rosewood, nestled in the heart of New England, love had a way of weaving its magic through the seasons. It was here that Emily Hart and Liam Clarke, two souls destined to find each other, discovered that love had a language all its own—one that transcended time and space.

Emily, with her cascade of curly auburn hair and eyes that sparkled like the stars, was a librarian with a passion for old books and the stories they held. She spent her days surrounded by the scent of aged paper and the whispers of forgotten times, her heart always attuned to the echoes of the past.

Liam, a tall and rugged man with a heart as vast as the New England sky, was a carpenter with a talent for restoring old houses to their former glory. His hands, rough and calloused from years of hard work, were capable of creating beauty from the remnants of time.

Their worlds collided on a rainy afternoon when Emily sought shelter in the antique shop next to Liam's workshop. As she browsed through the shelves, her eyes fell upon a dusty, leather-bound book titled "The Chronicles of Rosewood." Intrigued, she opened it to find pages filled with hand-written notes and sketches of the town as it once was.

The shopkeeper, a kind old man named Henry, noticed her interest and struck up a conversation. He explained that the book had belonged to his grandmother, who had lived in Rosewood for over eighty years. Emily was fascinated, and as she left the shop, she couldn't help but feel a strange connection to the place and its history.

A few days later, Emily found herself walking past Liam's workshop, drawn by the sight of an old house being restored to its former elegance. She stopped to watch, mesmerized by the way Liam's hands moved with precision and grace. He noticed her watching and smiled, inviting her to take a closer look.

From that moment on, Emily and Liam's bond began to grow. They spoke of their dreams, fears, and the stories that shaped them. Emily shared her love for old books and the magic they held, while Liam revealed his fascination with restoring the beauty of the past.

As they spent more time together, they discovered a shared passion for Rosewood and its history. They walked through the town's cobblestone streets, uncovering hidden gems and uncovering the stories of those who had once walked its paths. They visited the old library, where Emily worked, and spent hours poring over old maps and documents, searching for clues to the town's rich past.

One evening, as they sat on the porch of Emily's cozy cottage, sipping hot chocolate and watching the stars, Liam revealed a secret project he had been working on—a beautifully restored house on the outskirts of Rosewood. He had discovered it while restoring another house and had fallen in love with its charm and history.

Emily was moved beyond words. She had never felt so seen, so understood. She knew that this house, this place, was where they were meant to be. She reached out, her fingers tracing the outline of Liam's hand. "Liam," she whispered, "this... this is where we belong."

Liam smiled, his eyes reflecting the same depth of feeling. "I know, Emily. This house, this town... they're part of our story. They're the echoes of the past, calling us to create a future together."

From that night on, Emily and Liam's love became an enduring part of Rosewood's story. They restored the old house, transforming it into a cozy home filled with love and laughter. They continued to uncover the town's secrets, sharing their discoveries with the community and inspiring others to embrace the magic of the past.

As the years passed, Emily and Liam's bond grew stronger, their love echoing through the generations. They became beloved figures in Rosewood, their story passed down through the town's history, a testament to the timeless bond of love that had always been there, waiting to be discovered.

Story 7: A Love That Conquers All

In the bustling city of New York, where the skyline was a symphony of steel and glass, love often seemed like a fleeting whisper lost in the cacophony of urban life. Yet, for Alexandro "Alex" Carter and Isabella "Bella" Ramirez, love was not just a feeling but a force—a force that would conquer all obstacles that came its way.

Alex, with his dark, wavy hair and eyes that seemed to hold the mysteries of the universe, was a talented musician whose melodies had the power to soothe even the most troubled souls. He played the guitar with a passion that burned brightly, each note a testament to his unyielding spirit.

Bella, with her cascading waves of chestnut hair and eyes that sparkled with an inner fire, was a dedicated journalist whose words had the power to expose the truth and inspire change. She had a heart as fierce as her intellect, and a determination that knew no bounds.

Their worlds collided on a rainy evening at a small, dimly lit jazz bar in Manhattan. Alex was performing, his fingers dancing across the guitar strings, each note weaving a spell that captured the audience's attention. Bella, who had stumbled into the bar seeking shelter from the rain, was immediately drawn to the music. She found herself standing at the edge of the stage, her eyes locked on Alex as if he were the only person in the world.

From that moment on, they were inseparable. They spoke of their dreams, fears, and the world they wanted to create. Alex shared his passion for music, his belief that it had the power to heal and transform. Bella, in turn, revealed her commitment to journalism, her desire to shine a light on the darkness and inspire others to stand up for what was right.

As their relationship deepened, so did the challenges they faced. Alex's music career was on the rise, but with it came the pressures of fame and the demands of a relentless industry. Bella's job as a journalist often required her to travel to dangerous places, to face threats and danger in pursuit of the truth.

Their paths were often divergent, yet their love remained steadfast. They found ways to connect, even when separated by thousands of miles. Alex would send Bella heartfelt letters, his words a soothing balm for her weary soul. Bella, in turn, would send Alex articles she had written, her words a testament to their shared values and beliefs.

One particularly challenging period came when Bella was assigned to cover a story in a war-torn country. The danger was palpable, and Alex was worried sick. Yet, he knew that Bella had to do this, that her commitment to journalism was as deep as his commitment to music.

As Bella prepared to leave, Alex played her a song he had written especially for her. The melody was a blend of joy and sorrow, of hope and resilience. It was a song that captured the essence of their love, a love that knew no bounds, a love that would conquer all.

Bella listened, her eyes brimming with tears. She knew that no matter how far apart they were, no matter how difficult the journey, their love would guide them home.

When Bella finally returned, she was greeted by Alex's embrace, warm and strong. They stood together, a testament to the power of love. They knew that their journey was just beginning, that there would be more challenges to face, more obstacles to overcome. But they also knew that with each other, they could conquer anything.

And so, in the heart of New York City, where the skyline never slept and the streets were always bustling, Alex and Bella's love shone brightly, a beacon of hope and inspiration for all who believed in the magic of true love.

Story 8: A Love That Sparkles

In the picturesque town of Napa Valley, California, where vineyards stretched as far as the eye could see and the air was filled with the scent of ripe grapes, love had a way of sparkling like the finest champagne. For Emily Clarke and James Thompson, their love was not just a feeling, but a celebration—a celebration of life, of passion, and of the simple joys that make every moment worth living.

Emily, with her cascading waves of auburn hair and eyes that sparkled with an inner light, was a talented sommelier whose passion for wine knew no bounds. She had a nose for the finest blends and a palate that could discern the subtle nuances of even the most complex wines.

James, with his chiseled features and a smile that could light up even the darkest corners, was a successful entrepreneur whose love for Emily knew no limits. He had built a thriving business in the tech industry, but his heart belonged to the vineyards and the simple pleasures of life.

Their love story began on a sunny afternoon at a local wine festival. Emily was working a shift at a prestigious wine stand, her eyes scanning the crowd for potential customers. James, who had stumbled upon the festival by chance, was immediately drawn to Emily's passion and expertise.

As they tasted wines together, their conversation flowed easily, covering topics from the intricacies of wine production to their shared love for adventure and travel. By the end of the afternoon, it was as if they had known each other for a lifetime.

From that day on, Emily and James were inseparable. They explored the vineyards of Napa Valley, their fingers intertwined as they wandered through rows of grapevines, savoring the flavors of each new wine they discovered. They shared intimate picnics under the shade of oak trees, their laughter echoing through the vineyards like a melody of joy.

As their relationship deepened, so did their love for each other. They found joy in the smallest things, from watching the sunset over the vineyards to sharing a simple meal cooked at home. Each moment was a celebration, a testament to the fact that love, when truly felt, has the power to sparkle like the finest champagne.

One particularly special evening, James took Emily to a secluded vineyard he had discovered on one of his many explorations. As the sun dipped below the horizon, casting a golden glow over the vines, James proposed, his voice filled with emotion and sincerity.

Emily, tears of joy streaming down her cheeks, said yes. In that moment, their love felt as infinite as the sky, as timeless as the vineyards that surrounded them.

As they planned their wedding, they chose a vineyard as the venue, inviting friends and family to celebrate their love amidst the beauty of nature. The day was a symphony of joy, of laughter and music, of love and commitment.

Emily and James knew that their journey together was just beginning. They faced the challenges of life with grace and resilience, their love serving as a guiding light. Whether it was navigating the ups and downs of their careers or supporting each other through personal struggles, they did so with a sense of unity and purpose.

And so, in the heart of Napa Valley, where love sparkled like the finest champagne, Emily and James's love story continued to unfold, a celebration of life, of passion, and of the simple joys that make every moment worth living.

Story 9: A Love That Takes Flight

In the bustling city of New York, where the skyline was a canvas of steel and glass, love had a way of taking flight, transcending the chaos and finding a place to land amidst the hustle and bustle. For Alexandrowa "Lexi" Miller and Jackson "Jack" Harris, their love was not just a feeling, but a journey—a journey of discovery, of growth, and of finding each other amidst the endless possibilities that the city had to offer.

Lexi, with her wild, curly hair and eyes that seemed to hold the mysteries of the universe, was a free-spirited artist whose passion for painting knew no bounds. She had a way of capturing the essence of life in her work, whether it was the vibrant colors of a summer sunset or the quiet whispers of a city street.

Jack, with his chiseled jawline and a smile that could light up even the darkest corners of the city, was a driven entrepreneur whose ambition knew no limits. He had built a thriving business in the finance industry, but his heart belonged to the skies, to the freedom and adventure that only flying could provide.

Their love story began on a whim, a chance encounter in a crowded café on a rainy afternoon. Lexi was sketching the passersby, capturing the essence of the city in her notebook, while Jack was nursing a cup of coffee, lost in his thoughts.

As they struck up a conversation, their worlds collided in a whirlwind of passion and creativity. Lexi was fascinated by Jack's love for flying, his tales of soaring through the clouds and the endless horizon. Jack, in turn, was drawn to Lexi's vibrant spirit and her ability to see beauty in even the most mundane things.

From that day on, Lexi and Jack were inseparable. They explored the city together, their fingers intertwined as they wandered through the bustling streets, discovering hidden gems and making memories that would last a lifetime.

As their relationship deepened, so did their love for each other. Lexi found inspiration in Jack's ambition and drive, while Jack found peace and serenity in Lexi's creative spirit. They were a perfect balance, two halves of a whole that fit together seamlessly.

One particularly special evening, Jack took Lexi to a small, private airport outside the city. As the sun dipped below the horizon, casting a golden glow over the runway, Jack revealed his plan: to take Lexi on a private plane ride, to show her the world from a perspective she had never seen before.

Lexi, tears of joy streaming down her cheeks, eagerly accepted. As they soared through the clouds, the city below them shrinking to a mere speck on the horizon, Lexi felt a sense of freedom and adventure that she had never experienced before.

In that moment, as they held each other's hands and gazed out at the endless sky, Lexi and Jack knew that their love was something special, something that could take flight and transcend the boundaries of time and space.

As they continued their journey together, they faced the challenges of life with grace and resilience. Whether it was navigating the ups and downs of their careers or supporting each other through personal struggles, they did so with a sense of unity and purpose.

And so, in the heart of New York City, where love could take flight amidst the chaos and bustle, Lexi and Jack's love story continued to unfold, a journey of discovery, of growth, and of finding each other amidst the endless possibilities that the city had to offer.

Story 10: A Love Beyond Time

In the quaint little town of Evergreen, nestled in the heart of Vermont, lived a young woman named Clara Thompson. Clara was known for her radiant smile and her insatiable curiosity about the world. She worked at the local bookstore, "Timeless Tales," where she spent her days surrounded by stories of adventure, love, and mystery.

One crisp autumn day, Clara was organizing the shelves when a tall, distinguished man walked into the store. His name was Ethan Harris, a history professor from nearby Amherst College. Ethan had come to Evergreen to research the town's old, abandoned clock tower, rumored to hold secrets of the past.

From the moment their eyes met, Clara and Ethan felt an inexplicable connection. They spent hours talking, sharing their love for history and literature. Clara showed Ethan around Evergreen, pointing out the charming shops, cobblestone streets, and the breathtaking view of the Green Mountains.

As days turned into weeks, their friendship blossomed into something deeper. They discovered they had much more in common than a passion for books and history. Both were orphans, having lost their parents to tragic accidents when they were young. This shared experience brought them closer, creating a bond that transcended time itself.

One evening, Ethan invited Clara to dinner at a cozy, candlelit restaurant overlooking the town square. As they enjoyed a hearty meal and sipped on warm cider, Ethan took Clara's hand in his. "Clara," he began, his voice trembling, "I know we've only known each other for a short time, but I feel like I've known you forever. I want to spend every moment of my life exploring the world with you, uncovering its secrets, and sharing our dreams."

Clara's eyes filled with tears of joy. She had never felt so understood, so loved. "Ethan," she whispered, "I feel the same way. I've been waiting for someone to see me, to truly see me, for so long. You've made my heart feel like it's come home."

As winter descended upon Evergreen, covering the town in a blanket of snow, Clara and Ethan's love continued to grow. They spent countless hours in the clock tower, where Ethan was conducting his research. The old, dusty rooms echoed with their laughter and conversation, as if the tower itself was celebrating their love.

One snowy night, Ethan surprised Clara with a romantic proposal. He led her to the top of the clock tower, where they could see the entire town illuminated by the moonlight. "Clara," he said, "will you marry me? Will you spend forever uncovering the mysteries of life with me?"

Clara's heart swelled with happiness. She nodded, tears streaming down her cheeks, and Ethan slipped the ring onto her finger. They embraced, their love as timeless as the stories they cherished.

Their wedding was a simple, elegant affair, held in the same restaurant where Ethan had first confessed his love. The town of Evergreen came together to celebrate, their hearts warming with the joy of the new couple.

Years passed, and Clara and Ethan's love remained as strong as ever. They traveled the world together, uncovering its secrets and sharing their stories. They returned to Evergreen often, where they continued to explore the clock tower and relive the magical moments of their early days.

In their twilight years, as they sat on a bench overlooking the town square, holding hands and watching the leaves fall, Clara whispered to Ethan, "Do you remember when we first met, in that little bookstore?"

Ethan smiled, his eyes twinkling with love. "How could I forget? You were the light that brightened my world, the one who showed me that love truly is beyond time."

And so, Clara and Ethan's love endured, a testament to the power of true love that transcends the boundaries of time and space.

Story 11: Moonlit Promises

In the small coastal town of Seaside, Oregon, lived a young woman named Olivia Brown. Olivia was known for her infectious laughter and her love for the ocean. She spent her days working at the local art gallery, where she showcased her paintings of the moonlit shores and the waves crashing against the rocky cliffs.

One evening, as Olivia was closing up the gallery, she noticed a man standing outside, staring at her paintings with a thoughtful expression. His name was Noah Miller, a marine biologist who had recently moved to Seaside to conduct research on the local marine life.

Noah was taken by Olivia's talent and her passion for the ocean. They struck up a conversation, and soon found that they had much in common. Both loved the tranquility of the seaside, the sound of the waves, and the beauty of the moonlit nights.

As the weeks passed, Noah and Olivia's friendship grew into something deeper. They spent countless hours walking along the shore, watching the sunset, and sharing their dreams and aspirations. Noah was fascinated by Olivia's artwork, and she was captivated by his knowledge of the ocean and his dedication to protecting its creatures.

One moonlit night, Noah took Olivia to a secret spot on the cliffs, where they could see the entire coastline illuminated by the silvery glow of the moon. As they sat together, the waves crashing against the rocks below, Noah took Olivia's hand in his.

"Olivia," he began, his voice filled with emotion, "I've been holding something inside me for a long time. From the moment I saw your paintings, I was drawn to you. Your passion for the ocean, your creativity, your kindness... everything about you makes me feel like I've found something truly special. I want to spend every moment of my life exploring the world with you, uncovering its secrets, and creating our own moonlit memories."

Olivia's heart swelled with joy. She had never felt so understood, so loved. "Noah," she whispered, tears streaming down her cheeks, "I feel the same way. You've made my heart feel like it's come home. I want to spend forever with you, painting our moonlit promises and making them come true."

From that night on, Noah and Olivia's love flourished. They continued to explore the coastline together, watching the sunsets and moonrises, creating beautiful memories that would last a lifetime. Noah's research took him to different parts of the world, but no matter where he was, he always found his way back to Olivia and the beauty of Seaside.

One special night, as they sat on the cliffs under the moonlight, Noah surprised Olivia with a romantic proposal. He had created a beautiful collage of her paintings, each one representing a special moment they had shared. "Olivia," he said, "will you marry me? Will you spend forever creating moonlit promises with me?"

Olivia's heart raced with excitement. She nodded, tears of joy streaming down her face, and Noah slipped the ring onto her finger. They embraced, their love as strong and eternal as the ocean they both cherished.

Their wedding was a simple, elegant affair, held on the cliffs of Seaside, with the moonlight casting a magical glow over the ceremony. The town of Seaside came together to celebrate, their hearts warming with the joy of the new couple.

As they danced under the moonlight, Olivia whispered to Noah, "I love you, Noah. I always will."

Noah smiled, his eyes twinkling with love. "And I love you, Olivia. Our love is as eternal as the moon and the ocean. We'll make our moonlit promises come true, no matter what life throws at us."

And so, Noah and Olivia's love endured, a testament to the power of true love that shines brightly under the moonlight.

Story 12: The Pureness of Love

In the small town of Willowbrook, nestled in the rolling hills of Vermont, lived a young woman named Emily Hart. Emily was known for her kind heart and her love for nature. She spent her days working at a local organic farm, where she grew and harvested fresh produce for the community.

One summer day, Emily met a man named Ethan Miller. Ethan was a photographer who had come to Willowbrook to capture the beauty of the countryside. He was immediately taken by Emily's radiant smile and her passion for the land.

As they talked, Emily learned that Ethan had a deep appreciation for the environment and a desire to preserve its beauty. She was drawn to his genuine love for nature and his dedication to capturing its essence through his lens.

Their friendship blossomed over the course of the summer, with Ethan often visiting the farm to take photos of Emily working among the crops. They spent countless hours walking through the fields, talking about their dreams and aspirations, and sharing their love for the natural world.

Emily found herself falling in love with Ethan's kindness, his creativity, and his unwavering commitment to preserving the beauty of the earth. Ethan, too, was captivated by Emily's pure heart and her dedication to living a sustainable lifestyle.

One evening, as the sun set behind the hills and the sky was painted with hues of pink and orange, Ethan took Emily to a secret spot he had discovered on the outskirts of Willowbrook. It was a small, serene lake surrounded by lush trees and wildflowers. As they sat together on a blanket, watching the stars begin to twinkle in the sky, Ethan took Emily's hand in his.

"Emily," he began, his voice filled with emotion, "from the moment I met you, I knew that you were someone special. Your love for the land, your kindness, and your pure heart have touched my soul in a way that I never thought possible. I want to spend every moment of my life with you, exploring the beauty of the world and creating memories that will last forever."

Emily's heart swelled with joy. She had never felt so understood, so loved. "Ethan," she whispered, tears streaming down her cheeks, "I feel the same way. You have brought a new sense of purpose and joy to my life. I want to spend forever with you, preserving the beauty of the earth and creating a life filled with love and harmony."

From that night on, Ethan and Emily's love flourished. They continued to explore the natural beauty of Vermont together, taking photos, hiking, and enjoying the simple pleasures of life. They lived a life of simplicity and sustainability, focused on nurturing their relationship and preserving the environment.

As the years passed, Ethan and Emily's love grew stronger and deeper. They built a small, eco-friendly home on the outskirts of Willowbrook, where they lived surrounded by the beauty of nature. They welcomed a daughter, Lily, who inherited their love for the earth and their dedication to living a sustainable lifestyle.

Emily and Ethan's love was a testament to the pureness of love that transcends time and circumstance. They lived a life filled with joy, harmony, and a deep appreciation for the natural world. Their love was as strong and enduring as the hills of Vermont, a shining example of the beauty of true love.

Story 13: The Timeless Passion

In the bustling city of New York, amidst the towering skyscrapers and the endless hustle and bustle, lived a young woman named Clara Thompson. Clara was a talented artist, known for her ability to capture the essence of human emotion in her paintings. She spent her days in a small, sunlit studio in Manhattan, where she painted portraits of people from all walks of life.

One day, Clara met a man named Jackson Hayes. Jackson was a successful businessman who had recently moved to New York to take a new job. He was immediately drawn to Clara's vibrant spirit and her passion for her art.

As they talked, Clara learned that Jackson had a deep appreciation for the beauty of art and a desire to support creative endeavors. He was fascinated by Clara's ability to capture the intricate details of human emotion in her work. Clara, too, was taken by Jackson's intelligence, his kindness, and his genuine interest in her art.

Their friendship quickly blossomed into a deep and meaningful relationship. Clara and Jackson spent countless hours together, exploring the city, attending gallery openings, and discussing their dreams and aspirations. Clara painted portraits of Jackson, capturing the warmth and depth of his character in her work. Jackson, in turn, supported Clara's artistic endeavors, encouraging her to push her boundaries and explore new mediums.

As their relationship grew, Clara and Jackson found themselves falling deeply in love. They shared a bond that transcended time and circumstance, a connection that was as strong and enduring as the city itself.

One evening, as they sat together on the rooftop of Clara's building, watching the sun set over the city, Jackson took Clara's hand in his. "Clara," he began, his voice filled with emotion, "from the moment I met you, I knew that you were someone special. Your passion for your art, your kindness, and your vibrant spirit have touched my life in a way that I never thought possible. I want to spend every moment of my life with you, exploring the beauty of the world and creating memories that will last forever."

Clara's heart swelled with joy. She had never felt so understood, so loved. "Jackson," she whispered, tears streaming down her cheeks, "I feel the same way.

You have brought a new sense of purpose and joy to my life. I want to spend forever with you, painting our love story and creating a life filled with passion and harmony."

From that night on, Clara and Jackson's love flourished. They continued to explore the beauty of New York together, attending gallery openings, trying new restaurants, and enjoying the simple pleasures of life. Clara's art flourished under Jackson's encouragement, and she began to gain recognition for her work. Jackson, too, found new inspiration in Clara's passion for her art, and he pursued his own creative endeavors with renewed vigor.

As the years passed, Clara and Jackson's love grew stronger and deeper. They built a life filled with love, laughter, and a deep appreciation for the beauty of the world. They traveled to new places, experienced new cultures, and created memories that would last forever.

Clara and Jackson's love was a testament to the timeless passion that transcends time and circumstance. They lived a life filled with joy, harmony, and a deep appreciation for the beauty of the world. Their love was as strong and enduring as the city of New York, a shining example of the beauty of true love.

Story 14: Love at First Sight

It was a crisp autumn morning in New York City when Emily Johnson first laid eyes on him. She had always loved this time of year—the vibrant hues of red, orange, and yellow leaves against the crisp blue sky, the cool breeze that nipped at her cheeks, and the faint scent of cinnamon from the nearby bakery. Today, however, something magical was in the air.

Emily was standing at the corner of 5th Avenue and 57th Street, waiting for the traffic light to change. She was dressed in her favorite cozy sweater, a deep burgundy that complemented her hazel eyes, and her long auburn hair flowed freely around her shoulders. She had just come from a meeting at her advertising firm and was on her way to grab a coffee before heading back to the office.

As she stood there, her thoughts drifting, she noticed a man walking towards her from the opposite direction. He was tall, with broad shoulders and a confident stride. His hair was a tousled mess of dark brown waves, and his eyes—oh, his eyes—were a mesmerizing shade of green, sparkling with intelligence and warmth. He wore a charcoal grey suit that seemed to mold perfectly to his body, and a subtle hint of a smile played on his lips.

Emily felt her heart skip a beat. She couldn't tear her gaze away from him. It was as if the entire world had frozen in that moment, and there was only him. When the light finally changed, they both started walking, converging towards each other. As they passed, their eyes met, and for a fleeting second, it felt like time stood still.

Emily's mind raced. She wanted to say something, to acknowledge the connection she felt, but she was too shy. She watched him continue walking, her heart pounding in her chest. She turned around, hoping to catch another glimpse of him, and saw him entering a nearby café—the same one she had planned to go to.

On impulse, she quickened her pace and followed him inside. The café was warm and inviting, with the rich aroma of freshly brewed coffee filling the air. She scanned the room and saw him sitting at a corner table, a laptop open in front of him. She hesitated for a moment, but then, driven by an inexplicable force, she walked over to him.

"Excuse me," she said softly, her voice trembling. "Do you mind if I sit here?"

He looked up, his green eyes meeting hers again. For a moment, he seemed taken aback, but then a warm smile spread across his face. "Not at all," he replied, gesturing to the empty chair opposite him. "Please, have a seat."

Emily sat down, trying to calm her racing heart. She introduced herself, and he did the same. His name was Jack Thompson, and he was a software engineer working for a tech company nearby. They started talking, and Emily was amazed at how easily they connected. They shared stories about their lives, their dreams, and their passions. It felt like they had known each other for years, not minutes.

As they talked, Emily couldn't help but notice how Jack listened to her with such intensity, how his eyes lit up when he spoke about his work, and how his laughter filled the room. She felt an inexplicable pull towards him, a connection she had never felt before.

When their coffee was finished, they both knew they didn't want the moment to end. They decided to walk around the city, exploring the fall foliage and soaking in the ambiance. As they walked, their hands brushed against each other's accidentally, and they both paused, feeling the electricity that passed between them.

As the day wore on, Emily realized that she had fallen in love with Jack. It was love at first sight, a feeling she had never believed in but now knew existed. She felt a sense of peace and joy that she had never experienced before.

Jack, too, had felt the connection. He couldn't explain it, but he knew that Emily was someone special. He wanted to spend every moment with her, getting to know her better, exploring the depths of their connection.

As the sun began to set, casting a warm golden glow over the city, they found themselves standing in front of Central Park. They looked at each other, their eyes reflecting the beauty of the moment.

"Would you like to grab dinner with me?" Jack asked, his voice filled with hope.

Emily smiled, her heart swelling with happiness. "I'd love that," she replied.

They walked together into the park, hand in hand, their hearts beating in harmony. They knew that this was just the beginning of their journey, but they were ready to embrace it with all their hearts.

And so, in the heart of New York City, amidst the hustle and bustle of everyday life, two souls found each other, and love blossomed at first sight.

Story 15: The Perfect Match

In the bustling city of New York, amidst the towering skyscrapers and endless hum of traffic, lived two individuals whose paths were destined to intertwine. Emily Thompson, a young and ambitious journalist working for a renowned newspaper, had always believed in the magic of serendipity. Her days were filled with chasing deadlines, attending press conferences, and uncovering hidden stories, but her nights were often lonely, filled with dreams of meeting someone who could understand her passion and dreams.

Across the city, in Brooklyn Heights, lived Alex Martinez, a talented architect whose creativity knew no bounds. Alex's designs were renowned for their blend of modern aesthetics with a timeless charm. While his career flourished, his personal life remained somewhat stagnant. He had dated occasionally but had yet to find someone who resonated with him on a deep, intellectual level.

One crisp autumn evening, Emily received an assignment that would take her to a grand gallery opening in Manhattan. She dressed meticulously, choosing a sleek black dress that complemented her fiery red hair and emerald green eyes. As she arrived at the venue, she was immediately drawn to the exhibits, each piece telling a story that spoke to her soul.

Unbeknownst to her, Alex was also attending the same event. He had been invited to showcase his latest architectural designs, which were being featured prominently at the gallery. Alex was standing near a breathtaking glass sculpture, admiring its intricate details. His dark hair, sharp jawline, and intense hazel eyes caught Emily's attention as she wandered closer.

"That's quite impressive," Emily said, breaking the silence.

Alex turned, a smile playing on his lips. "Thank you. It's one of my favorites. Do you mind if I ask what you think of it?"

Emily was taken by his genuine curiosity and warmth. They began to discuss the piece, their conversation flowing naturally as they delved into their thoughts on art and creativity. Emily was fascinated by Alex's insights, and Alex was equally impressed by Emily's intelligence and passion for her work.

As the evening progressed, they found themselves gravitating towards each other, lost in conversation. They talked about their dreams, their fears, and the things that made them come alive. It was as if they had known each other for years, not mere hours.

The gallery began to empty, but neither Emily nor Alex noticed. They were too engrossed in each other's company. Finally, the gallery attendant's announcement that the event was closing brought them back to reality.

"I don't want this night to end," Emily admitted softly.

Alex took her hand in his, a gesture both bold and tender. "Neither do I. How about we continue this conversation somewhere else?"

Emily smiled, feeling a sense of connection she had never experienced before. "I'd like that."

They walked to a quaint little café nearby, where they ordered coffee and continued their conversation into the early hours of the morning. They laughed, shared stories, and found themselves amazed at how well they complemented each other.

As dawn approached, they finally bid each other goodnight, promising to meet again soon. Emily returned to her apartment, her heart racing with excitement and anticipation. Alex, too, felt a sense of elation, as if he had found a missing piece of himself.

Their relationship blossomed over the following weeks and months. They supported each other's careers, attended gallery openings and press conferences, and spent countless hours exploring New York City's hidden gems. They were a perfect match, not just in their interests and passions but in their hearts and souls.

One snowy winter evening, as they sat by the fireplace in Alex's cozy Brooklyn apartment, he took a deep breath and turned to Emily. "Emily, you have become the most important person in my life. I can't imagine my days without you. Will you marry me?"

Emily's eyes filled with tears of joy. "Yes, Alex. Yes, a thousand times yes."

Their wedding was a celebration of their love, attended by friends and family who had watched their relationship grow into something beautiful. They honeymooned in Paris, a city that embodied both their love for art and their romantic spirits.

Years passed, and Emily and Alex continued to grow together, their love only deepening with time. They had two children, who inherited their parents' creativity and passion for life. They remained a perfect match, not just in their love for each other but in their commitment to building a life filled with joy, purpose, and endless love.

And so, in the heart of New York City, amidst the endless hustle and bustle, Emily and Alex found their perfect match, a love story that proved that true connections can transcend time, space, and even the chaos of the city that never sleeps.

Story 16: A Boundless Love

In the quaint town of Maplewood, nestled amidst rolling hills and dense forests in the heart of Vermont, lived a young woman named Emma Thompson. Emma was known for her radiant smile and compassionate heart, always ready to lend a helping hand to anyone in need. She worked at the local library, a place that held a special place in her heart, surrounded by the warmth of books and the whispers of stories untold.

One crisp autumn afternoon, a new arrival in Maplewood caught Emma's eye. His name was Jack Miller, a charming and enigmatic man who had recently moved to the town to take up a position as a history professor at the nearby university. Jack had an air of mystery about him, his piercing blue eyes reflecting a depth of experiences and emotions that intrigued Emma from the very first moment she saw him.

Their paths crossed unexpectedly one evening at the annual Harvest Festival. The town square was adorned with twinkling lanterns and the air was filled with the scent of freshly baked pies and roasted chestnuts. Emma was helping organize a book giveaway, while Jack was simply wandering, taking in the serene beauty of Maplewood.

"Excuse me," Jack's voice interrupted Emma's thoughts as she carefully arranged a stack of books. "Could you recommend a good read?"

Emma turned to face him, her heart skipping a beat at the sight of his captivating smile. "Of course," she replied, her voice steady despite the flutter in her chest. "Do you have a particular genre in mind?"

They spent the next few hours lost in conversation, discussing books, their favorite authors, and their dreams and aspirations. Emma found herself drawn to Jack's intelligence and his passion for history, while Jack was captivated by Emma's warmth and her unwavering dedication to her community.

As the night drew to a close, Jack asked if he could walk Emma home. The moonlit path was serene, the crunch of leaves underfoot the only sound accompanying their steps. They talked and laughed, sharing stories of their pasts and hopes for the future. By the time they reached Emma's cozy cottage, it felt as though they had known each other for a lifetime.

From that evening on, Jack and Emma's bond grew stronger with each passing day. They spent countless hours together, exploring the serene trails of the Maplewood Forest, wandering through the quaint shops, and sharing quiet moments in the warmth of Emma's home. They discovered a shared love for classical music, spending evenings listening to symphonies and opera, their hearts resonating with the melodies.

As winter descended upon Maplewood, wrapping the town in a blanket of snow, Jack and Emma's relationship deepened. They found solace in each other's embrace, their love a beacon of warmth amidst the cold. On a snowy evening, as they sat by the fireplace, sipping hot chocolate and wrapped in each other's arms, Jack took Emma's hands in his.

"Emma," he began, his voice filled with emotion, "I've never felt anything like this before. You have brought a light into my life that I never knew existed. I love you, with all that I am and all that I will ever be."

Tears of joy welled up in Emma's eyes as she looked into Jack's loving gaze. "And I love you, Jack. My heart belongs to you, forever and always."

Their love was a testament to the boundless nature of true affection. It transcended time and space, a force that neither distance nor adversity could ever break. As they stood under the twinkling lights of the Maplewood town square on New Year's Eve, their hands entwined and their hearts beating in unison, they knew that they had found something truly special—a love that would withstand the test of time and remain as eternal as the stars above.

In the quiet corners of Maplewood, where love stories were often whispered among the leaves and the wind, Emma and Jack's tale became a legend. Their love was a beacon, a reminder to all who lived in the town that true love, once found, was a treasure to be cherished and protected, forever and always.

Story 17: The Sweetness of Your Kiss

In the charming town of Rosewood, nestled amidst lush green hills and sparkling rivers in the picturesque state of Oregon, lived a young woman named Lily Parker. Lily was known for her infectious laughter and her kindness, always ready with a smile and a listening ear for anyone who needed it. She worked at the local bakery, "Lily's Sweet Haven," a place that embodied the warmth and joy of her spirit, with its delicious aromas and the sound of baking bread filling the air.

One sunny morning, as Lily was arranging freshly baked cookies on display, a new customer walked into the bakery. His name was Ethan Hunt, a charming and enigmatic man who had recently moved to Rosewood to take up a position as a photographer for a local magazine. Ethan's eyes sparkled with curiosity and a hint of mischief, and his presence filled the bakery with an air of excitement that was palpable.

Lily's heart skipped a beat as she greeted Ethan, her cheeks flushing slightly as she handed him a menu. From the moment they met, there was an undeniable connection between them, a spark that seemed to ignite with every glance and every word exchanged.

As the days turned into weeks, Ethan became a regular at Lily's Sweet Haven. They spent countless hours together, talking and laughing, sharing stories of their pasts and dreams for the future. Lily found herself drawn to Ethan's creativity and his passion for photography, while Ethan was captivated by Lily's warmth and her unwavering dedication to her craft.

One evening, as the sun dipped below the horizon, casting a golden glow over Rosewood, Ethan invited Lily to join him on a sunset photo shoot at the nearby riverbank. Lily hesitated for a moment, her heart racing with a mix of excitement and nervousness, but she couldn't resist the opportunity to spend more time with Ethan.

As they walked along the riverbank, the world seemed to fade away, leaving only the two of them and the breathtaking beauty of the setting sun. Ethan took photo after photo, capturing the essence of the moment and the serene beauty of the landscape. But it was the photo he took of Lily, her face illuminated by the golden light of the sunset, that captured his heart forever.

As the sun dipped below the horizon, leaving the sky painted in hues of pink and orange, Ethan turned to Lily, his eyes filled with emotion. "Lily," he began, his voice soft and filled with sincerity, "there's something I've been wanting to say to you for a long time. You have brought so much light and joy into my life, and I can't imagine spending another day without you. I love you, Lily."

Lily's eyes widened in surprise, but her heart swelled with joy as she looked into Ethan's loving gaze. "Ethan," she replied, her voice trembling with emotion, "I love you too. More than I ever thought possible."

As they stood there, under the starlit sky, their hearts beating in unison, Ethan took Lily's hand in his and gently pulled her towards him. Their lips met in a tender kiss, sweet and pure, a kiss that encapsulated the depth of their love and the promise of a future filled with happiness and joy.

From that moment on, Lily and Ethan's love blossomed, growing stronger with each passing day. They spent countless hours together, exploring the beauty of Rosewood and the surrounding countryside, sharing quiet moments of intimacy and laughter. Their love was a testament to the sweetness of life and the power of true affection, a love that would withstand the test of time and remain as eternal as the stars above.

In the quiet corners of Rosewood, where love stories were often whispered among the leaves and the wind, Lily and Ethan's tale became a legend. Their love was a beacon, a reminder to all who lived in the town that true love, once found, was a treasure to be cherished and protected, forever and always.

Story 18: A Love That Heals

In the bustling city of Los Angeles, amidst the endless hustle and bustle of the urban landscape, lived a young woman named Emma Thompson. Emma was a nurse at St. Vincent's Hospital, a place where she had dedicated her life to helping others, bringing comfort and healing to those in need.

Emma was a compassionate and caring individual, always willing to go the extra mile for her patients. But despite her dedication to her work, Emma had been struggling with her own personal demons. A tragic accident in her past had left her with a broken heart and a lingering sense of loss that seemed impossible to overcome.

One evening, as Emma was walking through the hospital corridors, she came across a new patient named Jack Mitchell. Jack had been admitted to the hospital after a severe car accident that had left him with multiple injuries and a long road to recovery. Despite his physical pain, Jack's spirit remained unbroken, his eyes filled with determination and hope.

Emma took an immediate liking to Jack, and she found herself drawn to his positive outlook on life. She took charge of his care, making sure he had everything he needed to recover. As the days turned into weeks, Emma and Jack formed a strong bond, their conversations filled with laughter and shared stories of their pasts.

Emma found herself opening up to Jack, sharing the pain and sorrow of her own past. Jack listened intently, his presence a soothing balm that seemed to ease the ache in Emma's heart. In return, Jack shared his own story, the struggles he had faced and the triumphs he had overcome. Together, they found solace in each other's words, a sense of understanding and connection that transcended their physical wounds.

As Jack's physical injuries healed, so did Emma's broken heart. The love they shared was a powerful force, a healing balm that mended the wounds of their pasts and paved the way for a future filled with hope and joy. They supported each other through the ups and downs of Jack's recovery, their bond growing stronger with each passing day.

One sunny afternoon, as Jack was being discharged from the hospital, he turned to Emma, his eyes filled with gratitude and love. "Emma," he began, his voice filled with sincerity, "you have been my rock, my guiding light through this difficult time. I don't know what I would have done without you. I love you, Emma."

Emma's eyes filled with tears of joy as she looked into Jack's loving gaze. "Jack," she replied, her voice trembling with emotion, "I love you too. More than words can express. Together, we have found a love that heals, a love that will carry us through whatever life throws at us."

As they stood there, under the warm California sun, their hearts beating in unison, Emma and Jack knew that they had found something truly special. Their love was a testament to the power of healing, a love that would transcend time and space, a love that would remain eternal, forever and always.

In the bustling city of Los Angeles, where love stories were often overshadowed by the noise and chaos of daily life, Emma and Jack's tale became a beacon of hope. Their love was a reminder that true love, once found, had the power to heal even the deepest wounds, to bring joy and happiness to even the darkest corners of the world.

Story 19: The Serene Bliss of Love

In the picturesque town of Tahoe City, nestled in the heart of the Sierra Nevada mountains, lived a young woman named Sarah Johnson. Sarah was a talented painter, known for her ability to capture the beauty of nature on canvas. She had a deep love for the outdoors, often spending her days hiking, sketching, and painting the breathtaking landscapes that surrounded her.

One crisp autumn morning, as Sarah was setting up her easel by the shore of Lake Tahoe, she noticed a man walking along the beach, his gaze fixed on the shimmering waters of the lake. The man was named Ethan Miller, a software engineer who had recently moved to Tahoe City to escape the hustle and bustle of city life. He was taken by the serene beauty of the lake and the surrounding mountains, and he often found himself wandering along the shore, seeking peace and inspiration.

As Ethan approached Sarah, he couldn't help but be drawn to her quiet demeanor and the way she seemed to be in perfect harmony with the natural world. He introduced himself and struck up a conversation, and soon they found themselves sharing stories of their pasts and dreams for the future.

Sarah and Ethan discovered that they had much in common, a love for the outdoors, a passion for creativity, and a desire for a simpler, more fulfilling life. As the days turned into weeks, they spent more and more time together, exploring the beauty of Tahoe City and the surrounding area. They took long hikes through the mountains, paddled out on the lake in kayaks, and even tried their hand at rock climbing.

In each other's company, Sarah and Ethan found a sense of peace and contentment that they had never known before. They felt a deep connection, a bond that seemed to transcend the physical world and touch their souls. As they grew closer, they realized that they had found something truly special, a love that was serene, blissful, and filled with a sense of purpose.

One evening, as they sat by a crackling campfire under a starry sky, Ethan took Sarah's hand in his and looked into her eyes, filled with love and sincerity. "Sarah," he began, "I have never felt this way about anyone before. You bring a sense of peace and joy to my life that I never knew was possible. I want to spend every moment of my life with you, exploring this beautiful world and creating memories that will last a lifetime."

Sarah's eyes filled with tears of joy as she listened to Ethan's heartfelt words. "Ethan," she replied, her voice trembling with emotion, "I feel the same way. You have brought a sense of serenity and bliss to my life that I never thought I could find. I love you, Ethan, with all my heart."

As they sat there, surrounded by the beauty of nature and the warmth of their love, Sarah and Ethan knew that they had found something truly special. Their love was serene, filled with a sense of peace and contentment that seemed to flow through every fiber of their beings. They knew that together, they could face whatever life threw at them, with a love that was strong, enduring, and filled with a sense of purpose.

In the picturesque town of Tahoe City, Sarah and Ethan's love became a testament to the beauty of nature and the power of love. Their story was a reminder that true love, once found, could bring a sense of serenity and bliss that transcended the physical world and touched the soul. And as they continued to explore the beauty of the world together, Sarah and Ethan knew that their love would remain eternal, forever and always.

Story 20: The Heart's Secret

In the quaint town of Willowbrook, nestled between rolling hills and sparkling rivers in the heart of New England, lived a young woman named Clara Harris. Clara was known for her warm smile and the gentle way she carried herself, always with a book in hand and a song in her heart. She worked at the local library, a serene place filled with the scent of old paper and the whispered conversations of those seeking solace in words.

One crisp autumn afternoon, Clara was organizing a new shipment of books when a man walked into the library. His name was Ethan Miller, a recent transplant to Willowbrook after spending years in bustling New York City. Ethan was a journalist, sent to the small town to write a series of articles about its charm and history. He was tall, with disheveled hair and eyes that seemed to hold the weight of countless stories.

Clara noticed Ethan immediately. There was something about his presence that intrigued her, a quiet intensity that seemed out of place in their peaceful town. She greeted him with her usual warmth and helped him find some resources for his research. As days turned into weeks, Ethan frequented the library more often, always seeking Clara's guidance and engaging in long conversations about literature, philosophy, and the nuances of human behavior.

Unbeknownst to Clara, Ethan had become deeply captivated by her. He found himself drawn to her intelligence, her kindness, and the way her eyes sparkled when she talked about her passions. Clara, too, felt an inexplicable pull towards Ethan. She admired his curiosity, his dedication to his work, and the depth of his character. Yet, both were hesitant to admit their feelings, fearing the vulnerability that love often required.

One evening, as the library was closing, Ethan approached Clara with a sense of urgency he couldn't quite explain. "Clara," he began, his voice steady but his heart pounding, "there's something I need to tell you." Clara looked at him, her curiosity piqued. The library was empty, the only sound the gentle creak of the wooden floorboards under their feet.

Ethan took a deep breath and continued. "I've been writing these articles, trying to capture the essence of Willowbrook, but I realize now that the most important story I need to tell is my own. I've come to understand that this town, this library, and especially you, Clara, have brought something into my life that I didn't know I was missing—a sense of belonging, a reason to believe in the beauty of everyday moments."

Clara listened, her heart swelling with emotion. She had felt the same way but had been afraid to voice it. She reached out and touched Ethan's hand, feeling the warmth of his skin beneath hers. "Ethan," she said softly, "I've felt the same connection. It's like you've unlocked a part of me that I didn't even know existed. But I'm scared. Scared of getting hurt, scared of losing what we have if things don't work out."

Ethan smiled gently, his eyes reflecting the soft glow of the library lights. "I'm scared too, Clara. But I believe that sometimes, love is worth the risk. It's a journey, with ups and downs, but if we trust in ourselves and in each other, we can navigate it together."

Moved by his words, Clara nodded. "Then let's take this journey, Ethan. Together."

As they walked out of the library into the cool night air, hand in hand, they felt a sense of peace and excitement. They knew that their road ahead would not be without challenges, but they were ready to face them, armed with the knowledge that they had each other.

The Heart's Secret was not just the unspoken feelings that had grown between Clara and Ethan, but the courage it took to reveal them. In Willowbrook, surrounded by the simple beauty of nature and the unwavering support of their newfound community, they learned that love, like the pages of a well-loved book, was meant to be explored, cherished, and lived fully.

And so, Clara and Ethan's story unfolded, one chapter after another, filled with the laughter, tears, and endless wonder that true love brings.

Milton Keynes UK
Ingram Content Group UK Ltd.
UKHW051833011224
451808UK00011B/115

9 798887 544533